PLAYFUL PIGS from A to Z

Anita Lobel

Alfred A. Knopf
New York

One golden morning,
26 playful pigs woke up.
"What a day," they oinked as one.
"A fine day to go exploring!"

The 26 playful pigs left their pen and raced
along a country road. Just beyond a bend,
they came upon a field of magical surprises.

Amanda Pig admired an A.

Billy Pig balanced on a B.

Clara Pig cleaned a C.

Denzel Pig drew a D.

Erin Pig examined an E.

Floyd Pig fell by an F.

Greta Pig guarded a G.

Hugo Pig hugged an H.

Imogen Pig imitated an I.

Johnny Pig jogged around a J.

Kate Pig knitted near a K.

Lola Pig labeled an L.

Margo Pig memorized an M.

Ned Pig nibbled an N.

Oliver Pig observed an O.

Philip Pig pushed a P.

Quentin Pig questioned a Q.

Rosie Pig rescued an R.

Sarah Pig serenaded an S.

Timmy Pig trumpeted to a T.

Uma Pig unveiled a U.

Victor Pig vacuumed a V.

Wanda Pig watered a W.

Xavier Pig expected Xmas with an X.

Yolanda Pig yawned at a Y.

Zeke Pig zzz'd on a Z.

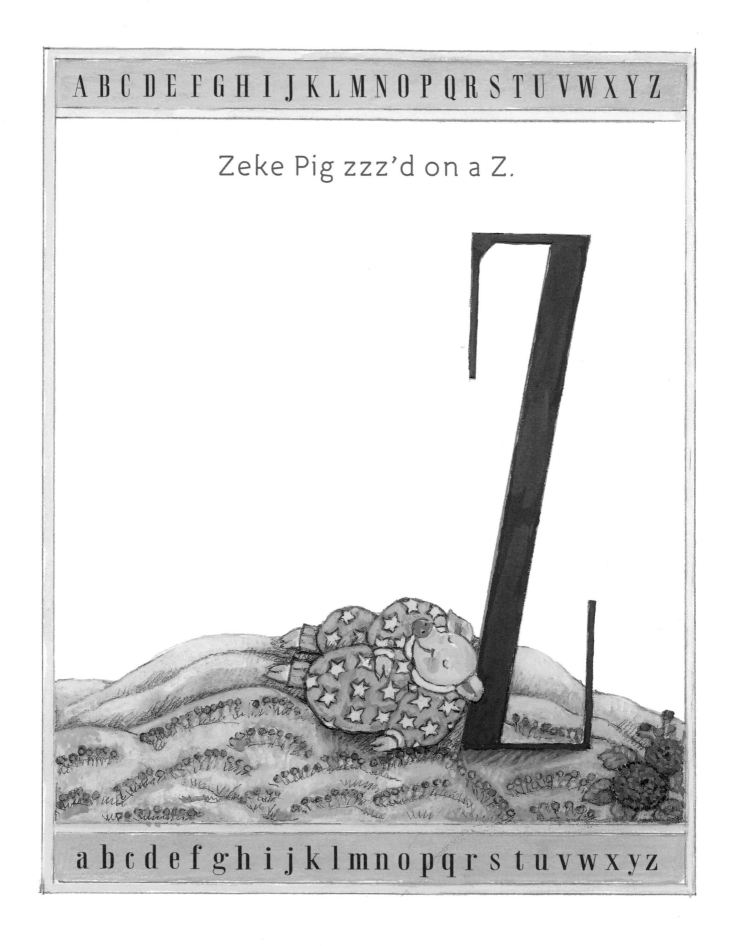

ABCDEFGHIJKLMNOPQRSTUVWXYZ

The moon rose in the sky as the 26 hungry and tired—but very happy—playful pigs ran home.

abcdefghijklmnopqrstuvwxyz

They ate their apples and corn and lay down in the hay. "Good night, good night," the pigs oinked sleepily.

"What an exciting day we had!
We learned the alphabet from A to Z."
The playful pigs slept well, knowing that
tomorrow was another day.

A B C D E F G H I J K L M N O P Q R S T U V W X Y Z

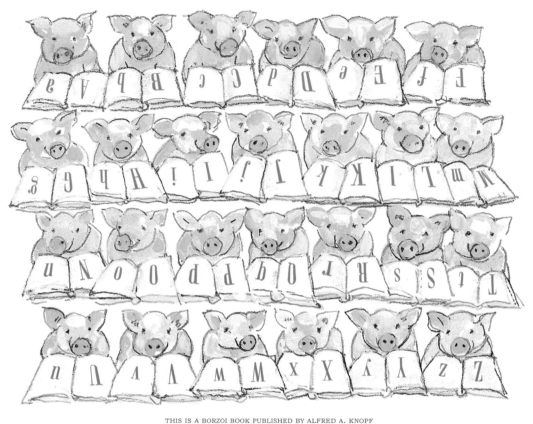

THIS IS A BORZOI BOOK PUBLISHED BY ALFRED A. KNOPF

Copyright © 2015 by Anita Lobel

All rights reserved. Published in the United States by Alfred A. Knopf,
an imprint of Random House Children's Books, a division of Random House LLC, a Penguin Random House Company, New York.
Knopf, Borzoi Books, and the colophon are registered trademarks of Random House LLC.

Visit us on the Web! randomhousekids.com

Educators and librarians, for a variety of teaching tools, visit us at RHTeachersLibrarians.com

Library of Congress Cataloging-in-Publication Data

Lobel, Anita, author, illustrator.

Playful pigs from A to Z / Anita Lobel. — First edition.

p. cm.

Summary: One golden morning, twenty-six pigs leave their pen, race along a country road, and find a field of letters, where they play
all day until Zeke Pig falls asleep on a Z and they wearily return home by moonlight.

ISBN 978-0-553-50832-1 (trade) — ISBN 978-0-553-50833-8 (lib. bdg.) — ISBN 978-0-553-50834-5 (ebook)

[1. Pigs—Fiction. 2. Play—Fiction. 3. Alphabet.] I. Title.

PZ7.L7794Pl 2015

[E]—dc23

2014033874

The text of this book is set in 22-point Roice.

The illustrations were created using gouache and watercolor.

MANUFACTURED IN MALAYSIA

July 2015

10 9 8 7 6 5 4 3 2 1

First Edition

Random House Children's Books supports the First Amendment and celebrates the right to read.

a b c d e f g h i j k l m n o p q r s t u v w x y z